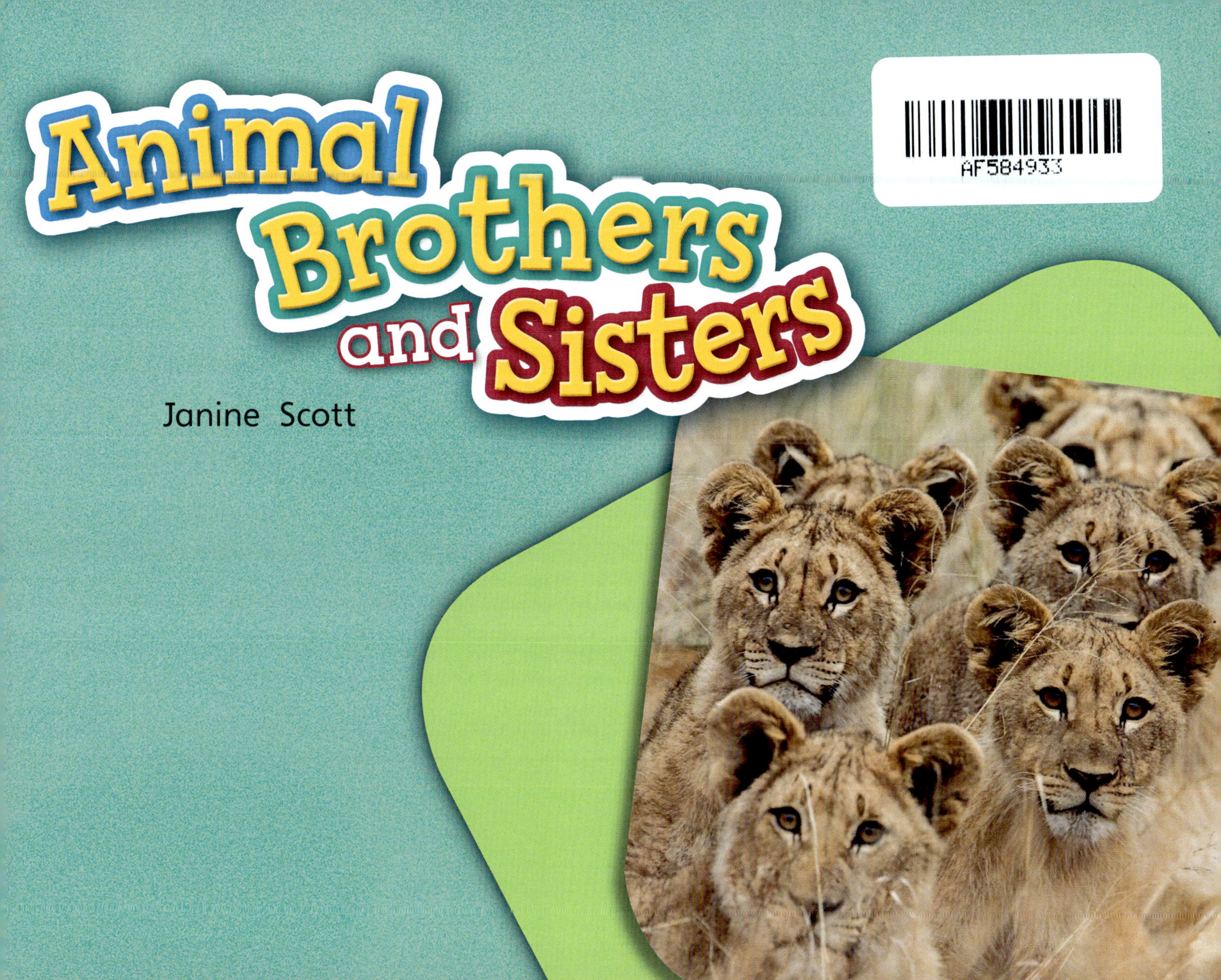
Animal Brothers and Sisters
Janine Scott
AF584933

Some baby animals have brothers and sisters. They are born at the same time.

Baby cheetahs have brothers and sisters.

Some animals have two babies.
These polar bears were born at the same time.

These deer were born at the same time, too.

Some animals have three babies.
These baby sheep are brothers and sisters.

These baby bears are brothers and sisters, too. They walk in a line behind their mother.

Some animals have lots of brothers and sisters. This mother lion has five babies.

This mother duck has nine babies.

Mother alligators have lots of babies.
These alligators ride on their mother's back.

Spiders have lots of brothers and sisters. Mother spiders can have hundreds of babies!

Baby elephants have brothers and sisters.
They are not born at the same time.

A baby emperor penguin has no brothers or sisters, but it has...

...lots of friends!

Baby Animal Names

Alligator: hatchling	Elephant: calf
Bear: cub	Lion: cub
Cheetah: cub	Penguin: chick
Deer: fawn	Sheep: lamb
Duck: duckling	Spider: spiderling